The week before that, a very tall building suddenly got in Winnie's way. Wilbur lost a clump of fur.

'The sky is too dangerous, Wilbur,' said Winnie. 'We'll have to try something else.' So she took our her wand, waved it, and shouted,

Abracadabra!

Her broomstick turned into a skateboard.
The skateboard was fast.
But it was hard to steer.
And impossible to stop.

Winnie was stopped. By an ice-cream seller.
'Can't you see where you're going?'
he shouted.

'A skateboard is worse than a broomstick, Wilbur,'
said Winnie. 'We'll have to try something else.'
So she took out her wand, waved it, and shouted,

Abracadabra!

Her skateboard turned into
a bicycle. But it was very slow.
Very hard to pedal.

And then a pond got in Winnie's way.
'She should look where she's going,' croaked a frog.

'A bicycle is worse than a skateboard, Wilbur,'
said Winnie. 'I think we'll walk home.'

They limped slowly along the road.
It was a very very slow way to travel.

But it was safe.

Until Winnie stepped into a hole and tumbled deep down under the ground.

YES WE ARE OPEN

'I think I need a cup of tea,' Winnie said.

Winnie climbed out of the tunnel
and went into a shop.

'A cup of tea and a muffin, please,' she said.
'And a saucer of milk for my cat.'

'We don't sell cups of tea or muffins,' said the shop lady. 'And we don't have saucers of milk. But I think I can help you.'

And she sold Winnie a pair of spectacles.

Now, Winnie and Wilbur travel everywhere by broomstick.

It's a wonderful way to travel.

# Winnie celebrates her 25th anniversary in 2012.

## Shown here (and on the back cover) are all her adventures for you to collect.

OXFORD
UNIVERSITY PRESS

Great Clarendon Street, Oxford OX2 6DP

Oxford is a registered trade mark of Oxford University Press
in the UK and in certain other countries

Text © Valerie Thomas 1999, 2012
Illustrations © Korky Paul 1999, 2012

The moral rights of the author/illustrator have been asserted

Database right Oxford University Press (maker)

First published in 1999
This World Book Day Edition first published in 2012

British Library Cataloguing in Publication Data

Data available

ISBN: 978-0-19-275838-5

2 4 6 8 10 9 7 5 3 1

Printed in Singapore

Paper used in the production of this book is a natural, recyclable product made
from wood grown in sustainable forests. The manufacturing process conforms
to the environmental regulations of the country of origin.

This book has been specially published for World Book Day 2012.
For further information please see www.worldbookday.com

World Book Day in the UK and Ireland is made possible by generous sponsorship
from National Book Tokens, participating publishers, authors and booksellers.

Booksellers who accept the £1 World Book Day Token bear the full cost of redeeming it.

www.korkypaul.com